For Doodle, who fears not — L. G.- B.

For my family — B. L.

Text copyright © 1996 by Lynda Graham-Barber
Illustrations copyright © 1996 by Barbara Lehman

First paperback edition in this format 2006

Library of Congress Catalog Card Number 95-071366

ISBN-10 0-7636-2911-1
ISBN-13 978-0-7636-2911-3

2 4 6 8 10 9 7 5 3 1

Printed in China

This book was typeset in Maiandra.

Candlewick Press
2067 Massachusetts Avenue
Cambridge, Massachusetts 02140
visit us at www.candlewick.com

Say Boo!

Lynda Graham-Barber

illustrated by **Barbara Lehman**

CANDLEWICK PRESS
CAMBRIDGE, MASSACHUSETTS

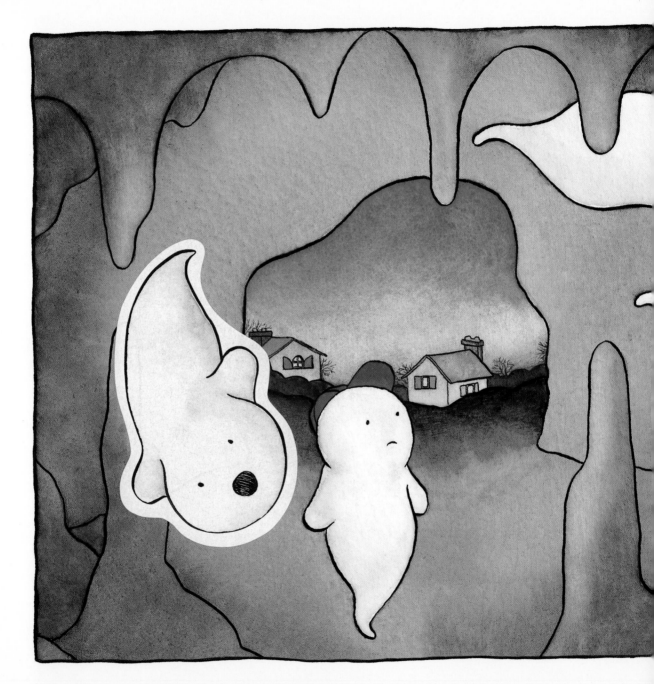

Ben watched his brothers and sisters swoop through the cave, shrieking and howling. But he didn't join them.

All week long, Ben had stood in front of the
mirror, puckering his lips. As hard as he tried,
the little ghost couldn't say "Boo."

*Who's ever heard of a ghost who can't say
"Boo"?* he thought.

With a whoosh, Ben's brother Boris landed beside him. "C'mon, Ben," he said. "Tonight's Halloween and you haven't even scared anyone yet."

"I know," Ben said with a sigh.

Sadly, Ben flew far into the forest, where
no one would hear him practice.

He sat in a tree, took a deep breath,
and puckered his lips. "Whooo!" Ben's voice
bounced off the tall pine trees.

Whooo!

"Whoo-whoo, yourself," said a high, clear voice. Ben looked up and saw a large owl sitting on a branch. "Owls say 'Whoo,'" said the owl. "You're supposed to say 'Boo.'"

"I know," Ben said, and he flew out of the
forest and into a meadow, where he tried again.
Ben took a deep breath, puffed up his chest,
and puckered his lips. "Mooo!" he bellowed.

"Moo-moo, yourself," said a low, deep voice. Peering at Ben through the lush green grass was a cow. "Cows say 'Moo,'" it said. "You're supposed to say 'Boo.'"

"I know," Ben said. *I'll never be a scary Halloween ghost*, he thought. Ben flew off and came to a long stone bridge. There he stopped, took his deepest breath ever, and puckered his lips. "Cooo!" he wailed.

"Coo-coo, yourself," came a soft, sweet voice. A bird in a nest under the bridge ruffled its feathers and said, "Doves say 'Coo.' You're supposed to say 'Boo.'"

"It's no use," Ben said, and began to cry.

Ben flew back to the forest, crying. Suddenly,
a brown bat swooped down and landed on his
shoulder.

"Boo-hoo, boo-hoo," the bat mocked him.
"What's this — a scary ghost crying on Halloween?"

"Boo-hoo, yourself," Ben mumbled. "Boo-hoo, boo-hoo, boo — Hey! I said 'Boo'!" he shouted. "Boo! Boo! Boo!"

"Eek!" squeaked the bat, and it flew off, trembling.

"Boo-boo, scaredy-bat!" Ben shouted after it.

Boo!

That Halloween night, when Ben joined Boris and all the other ghosts, his "Boo" was the scariest of all!

Lynda Graham-Barber is the author of twelve books, ten of which are for children. She lives on the Vermont-Quebec border with her artist husband and two rescued dogs. It was there, by lantern light, that she first saw little Ben, who wanted his story told.

Barbara Lehman was born in Chicago and raised in New Jersey. She studied illustration at Pratt Institute in Brooklyn and now lives in upstate New York. She has illustrated many picture books, including the alphabet book *Abracadabra to Zigzag*—the art for which was exhibited at a Society of Illustrators Original Art Show—and *Moonfall*, which won a Parents' Choice Award. She is also the author and illustrator of the wordless picture book *The Red Book*, which won a Caldecott Honor.